WAS KIN
F TAR

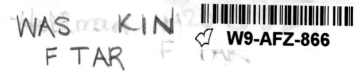

I SURVIVED

THE GREAT CHICAGO FIRE, 1871

by Lauren Tarshis

illustrated by Scott Dawson

Scholastic Inc.

For Stefanie Dreyfuss, my friend

Text copyright © 2015 by Lauren Tarshis
Illustrations copyright © 2015 by Scholastic Inc.
All rights reserved. Published by Scholastic Inc., *Publishers since 1920*.
SCHOLASTIC and associated logos are trademarks and/or
registered trademarks of Scholastic Inc.

ISBN 978-0-545-65846-1

35 34 33 32 31   22/0

Printed in the U.S.A.   40
First printing, March 2015
Designed by Yaffa Jaskoll
Series design by Tim Hall

CHAPTER 1

SUNDAY, OCTOBER 8, 1871
11:30 P.M.
CHICAGO

The fire started inside a barn.

It was tiny at first, a glowing dot, some wisps of white smoke.

But then flames reached up.

They grabbed hold of a pile of hay.

Crackle!

Pop!

And then,

1

Boom!

Towers of flame shot up, higher, higher, punching through the roof, reaching for the sky.

Voices screamed out.

"Fire! Fire! Fire!"

Alarm bells clanged. Firefighters readied their horses and raced their pumpers through the streets.

But it was too late.

The flames blasted a shower of fiery sparks into the windy sky. Like a swarm of flaming wasps, they flew through the air, starting fires wherever they landed. Shops and homes erupted in flames. Warehouses exploded. Mansions burned.

Crowds of panicked people fled their houses and rushed through the streets and along the wooden sidewalks. They screamed and pushed and knocked one another down, desperate to get away from the choking smoke and broiling flames.

But there was no escape.

The winds blew harder. Flames shot hundreds of feet in the air, spreading across miles and miles.

And in the middle of it all was eleven-year-old Oscar Starling.

Oscar had never felt so terrified, not even two years ago, when a killer blizzard hit his family's Minnesota farm.

He was trapped inside a burning house, fighting for his life. He'd made it down the stairs, desperate to escape. And then,

Crash!

A ball of fire and cinders crashed through the window, and the house exploded in flames. And suddenly, Oscar was in the fire's ferocious grip. The flames clawed at him, seared him, threw him to the ground. Smoke gushed up his nose and into his mouth. But the worst was the blistering heat, the feeling of being roasted alive.

Was this the end?

Oscar had never wanted to come to this city.

And now he was sure he was going to die here.

CHAPTER 2

THREE HOURS EARLIER
A TRAIN TO CHICAGO

Don't puke.

That's what Oscar had been telling himself for the past nine hours as the train chugged and swayed and jerked its way toward Chicago. They'd crossed four hundred miles of wide open prairie. For hours, Oscar had been staring out the window. There had been nothing to see but shoulder-high grass and a few scrawny buffalo that seemed

4

to wave good-bye to Oscar with their swishing tails.

Now that they were getting closer to the city, Oscar couldn't bear to look. He slouched down in his seat and glued his eyes to his dusty boots.

"Are you feeling all right, Oscar?" Mr. Morrow said.

"I'm fine, sir," Oscar lied.

"Such a long trip," Mama said, her freckled face shining with excitement. "I feel like we're heading up to the moon!"

Mama and Mr. Morrow both laughed, but nothing seemed funny to Oscar. So much had happened these past few weeks. He was in a state of shock. Mama had married Mr. Morrow. They had sold the Minnesota farm where Oscar had lived his entire life. And now they were moving to a strange city that might as well be the moon.

No wonder Oscar felt sick.

Of course the real nightmare had happened two years ago, when Papa died.

He was killed in a vicious blizzard, a wall of ice and snow and wind that slammed into their prairie town with no warning. Papa had been trying to get home. His wagon crashed into a tree in the blinding snow.

Even now, Oscar couldn't believe that Papa was gone.

Papa was the toughest man Oscar knew. He'd been a sheriff in Dakota Territory. He'd survived a gunfight with one of the most brutal outlaws in the West. He'd carved a farm out of forty acres of wild prairie.

Papa was Oscar's hero.

Those first weeks after Papa died, Oscar was sure his sadness would rip him apart. But he couldn't just lie in bed sobbing. With Papa gone, it was Oscar's job to help Mama with the farm. He made a whispered promise to Papa — to watch over the farm, to work as hard as he could to keep it going.

He worked before dawn and after school. He worked so hard he'd fall into bed every night, too exhausted to think.

Mama wanted Oscar to see his friends.

"Maybe tomorrow," Oscar always answered.

"Then come sit with me awhile," Mama would say. "Let's play cards."

He and Mama and Papa used to play fierce games of hearts. When Papa lost, he'd pretend to fly into a rage, pounding the table while Mama and Oscar doubled over laughing.

But Oscar had no time for cards. All he wanted to do was work.

The seasons passed in a blur of sweat and dirt and aching muscles.

And Oscar would have just kept on going. But then, six months ago, Mr. Charlie Morrow appeared at their door.

Mr. Morrow was an artist for a big Chicago newspaper. He'd come to Castle for his latest project, which was to paint scenes of life in a booming little prairie town. Mama was honored when Mr. Morrow stopped by and asked if he could paint their farm.

Each morning for a month, Mr. Morrow would show up just after the sun rose, waving at Mama and Oscar with his paint-stained fingers. "Hello!" he'd sing out.

He was a big man, with jet-black hair and a beard to match. Mama said he reminded her of a giant from a fairy tale. "But the nice kind," she explained.

Oscar liked Mr. Morrow well enough. He made Mama smile, that was for sure.

Most nights after Mr. Morrow packed up his paints, he'd join them for supper. Afterward he and Mama would sit out on the porch and look over the day's paintings.

"Oscar, join us," Mr. Morrow would boom.

But why did Oscar need to look at paintings of his farm? He lived there!

So he'd make excuses and then fall asleep to the sound of Mr. Morrow and Mama's soft laughter drifting upstairs. After Mr. Morrow went back to Chicago, Mama seemed to get a letter from him every single day.

So maybe Oscar shouldn't have been shocked when, two months ago, Mama sat Oscar down under the apple tree with some big news.

"He's asked me to marry him," she said.

At first Oscar laughed.

Mr. Morrow? He was nothing like Papa! He was an artist. An artist! Was that even a job?

But then Oscar noticed how Mama's eyes were twinkling.

"Oscar," she said. "I want to say yes."

Oscar stopped laughing.

"He's a wonderful man," she said. "And what a life we'll have with him in Chicago."

At first Oscar just sat there like he'd been smacked in the head with a shovel.

Leave the farm? Move to Chicago?

What about his promise to Papa?

Oscar begged Mama. He pleaded with her. He tried to make her understand that they needed to stay in Castle.

"Papa wouldn't want us to leave here!" he exclaimed.

But then Mama looked at Oscar with her hopeful eyes.

"Oscar," she said quietly, putting her hand up to Oscar's cheek. Her fingers were like Oscar's, covered with calluses and scars from all the scrubbing and weeding and washing that filled her days. "All Papa ever wanted was for us to be happy."

And Oscar could see that she had made up her mind.

Oscar could have run away, or refused to get on the train.

But he didn't have the guts.

So now here he was, miserable, chugging along with his stomach turning inside out.

The train whistle shrieked.

Woooooo! Wooooooo!

"Chicago!" the conductor shouted out. "Ten minutes!"

Oscar's stomach flipped.

Don't puke!

His stomach didn't listen.

He managed to slam open the window just in time to splatter his lunch across the tracks.

Welcome to Chicago.

CHAPTER 3

Oscar stared out the window in shock as the train pulled into the city.

Chicago was called the Queen of the West.

But what an ugly queen!

All along the tracks were factories and warehouses. The sky was smudged dirty brown from coal fires and dark clouds burping out of smokestacks.

Soon enough, they were off the train and standing in the enormous station hall. Every other person smiled and waved at Mr. Morrow.

"Charlie!" a man boomed.

"Welcome back, Mr. Morrow," said a porter lugging a heavy suitcase.

"Mr. Morrow, I loved your latest pictures!" a pretty woman gushed.

"Good to be back!" Mr. Morrow beamed.

People swarmed around the station — more people than Oscar had seen in all of his life. Everyone was rushing around as if they were late for church.

And suddenly, Oscar noticed the rotten stench that filled the air. He had never smelled anything as disgusting. It was like someone had tossed a hundred skunks into a hot outhouse and left them there for a month.

Oscar could see from Mama's crinkled-up nose that she noticed it, too.

"The slaughterhouses," Mr. Morrow said, reading their sickened expressions. "They butcher more hogs in Chicago than anywhere in the world."

Mr. Morrow went to the baggage room and returned with their three suitcases. Oscar's was the smallest. Inside was all that was left from his life on the farm: his few clothes and his prized possession — Papa's sheriff's badge, a five-pointed silver star.

"Is there somewhere I can freshen up?" Mama asked, smoothing one of the golden curls that had popped out of her bun.

"I'll show you," Mr. Morrow said, taking Mama's arm. "Oscar, can you keep an eye on the bags?"

Oscar nodded.

But as they disappeared into the crowd, Oscar's heart thumped.

He felt so out of place here, and strangely all alone. A bunch of rough-looking boys lurked around. One of them stared at Oscar. He had bright red hair and strange yellow-tinged eyes that reminded Oscar of a rattlesnake's. Oscar was relieved when they drifted away.

He took a deep breath and looked around, thinking about Papa's one visit to Chicago. Papa was just twenty years old at the time. His parents had both died, and Papa had decided to leave his hometown near Boston and head west.

"I was looking for my fortune," Papa always said.

He landed in a no-name town in Dakota Territory. The town was desperate for a sheriff, and Papa needed a job. For months the place was quiet — until the night a gang of outlaws rode in.

Their leader was Earless Max Kildair.

"Actually, Earless did have one ear," Papa had explained to Oscar. "He lost the left one blowing up a safe during a bank robbery."

Papa heard that Earless Kildair was a killer. And sure enough, by morning the town's bank had been robbed, and one of Papa's friends was sprawled out dead in the street. Earless and his gang were long gone.

Papa went after the gangster, chasing him all the way to Chicago. He finally found him in a stinking tavern near the river. Papa pulled out his gun, ready to arrest him. But Earless was too quick. He jumped behind the bar and started shooting.

Pow!

A bullet whizzed just past Papa's head.

Pow!

Papa fired back but missed.

Earless lunged forward with a final shot.

Pow!

The bullet hit Papa in the chest. It should have torn a hole right through Papa's heart. But it ricocheted off his badge instead, leaving a big dent smack-dab in the center.

Earless escaped in the commotion.

After that, Papa decided he was done chasing outlaws. He heard about free farmland up for grabs in Minnesota. He'd never farmed, but figured he'd give it a try. He ended up in a little town called Castle, where the first person he met was a freckle-faced schoolteacher with the prettiest blue eyes Papa had ever seen.

Mama.

Within the month, they were married. By the next year they had their farm — and Oscar.

"So I found my fortune," Papa liked to say, kissing Mama on the cheek.

As for Earless, he was still on the loose. Papa heard he was in Chicago, lying low, but still up to no good.

Oscar's thoughts of Papa were cut short by a whispering voice.

"Can you help me?"

He looked down at a skinny little girl with a yellow cap over two raggedy braids. She stared up at him with big brown eyes.

"I've lost my parents."

She looked so helpless!

"We'll find them," Oscar said, standing a little taller.

"I think they went this way," she said, leading him by the arm out of the main waiting room.

But then suddenly she let go of his sleeve.

"Sorry," she said.

And then *poof*, she disappeared into the crowd.

An uneasy feeling grabbed hold of Oscar.

Something wasn't right.

He spun around and rushed back to the suitcases.

They were gone.

CHAPTER 4

THIRTY MINUTES LATER
9:00 P.M.
ILLINOIS CENTRAL TRAIN DEPOT

"Those street kids are vicious," the policeman said. He looked down at Oscar. "Son, you're lucky you didn't get stabbed."

Mama, Mr. Morrow, and Oscar stood with the policeman on the spot where their suitcases had been. The cop, Officer Brennan, was an old buddy of Mr. Morrow's. He explained that Oscar had been tricked. That little girl wasn't really lost. She was a crook, part of a band of thieves.

"She distracted you so the others could steal the suitcases," Officer Brennan said. "Happens here every day."

Officer Brennan and three other cops had already scoured the station, but there was no sign of the girl or the bags or those rough boys Oscar had seen. Oscar told the policeman about them, too, including the redheaded boy with the strange eyes.

"Otis Webber," the cop said, his friendly eyes narrowing. "He's only fourteen years old, but he's got the heart of a killer. We hear he works for an older guy. They take helpless orphans and turn them into ruthless criminals."

Oscar shuddered.

"Will you find our suitcases?" Mama said.

"Doubtful, ma'am," he said, giving them all an apologetic smile before he left.

Mr. Morrow put his arm around Oscar's shoulders. "I should have warned you," he said. "In a big city like this, there are some bad characters."

"What's done is done," Mama said, shaking the worry from her face. "We can all get new clothes. What matters is that here we are, together."

Mr. Morrow beamed at Mama.

Oscar ducked out from under Mr. Morrow's arm.

Oscar didn't care about his clothes. All he cared about was Papa's badge, which was gone forever.

It was past 10:00 P.M. when they finally got out of the station and into a cab, a beat-up buggy pulled by a dusty horse. The cabdriver flashed a smile filled with black teeth when he saw Mr. Morrow.

"Charlie!" he cried. "Welcome back!"

Was there anyone in Chicago who didn't know Mr. Morrow?

"Hello, Joseph!" Mr. Morrow said, patting the man on the shoulder. "Take us to the Palmer House, please."

Joseph let out a sharp whistle. "Fancy!"

"We'll have supper there," Mr. Morrow told Mama and Oscar. "Then we'll head home. Oscar,

I think you're going to like the house. My father built it. It's a little far away from things, north of our new park. The best room is my studio. You can look out the windows and see all of Chicago."

Oscar managed a nod and bit his tongue.

Mr. Morrow's house would never be home. Home was Papa's farm, where the air didn't smell like dead hogs, where the only thieves were the rabbits that stole carrots from the garden.

The horse clattered away from the train tracks and warehouses and onto a wide avenue of grand buildings. Oscar tried not to act like he was impressed, but the buildings were taller than any tree he'd ever climbed.

"Amazing, isn't it?" Mr. Morrow said, smiling proudly. "When I was born, this city was just a little town on a marsh. Today, Chicago is one of the most important cities in the world."

"It's beautiful," Mama said.

But suddenly Mama's expression darkened.

"Does the sky look odd to you?" she asked, her brow wrinkling with worry.

Oscar saw it, too, a pale orange glow in the sky.

"Must be a fire," Joseph said matter-of-factly. "We're having fires practically every night now. Hasn't rained here in months. The city is bone-dry."

The word *fire* sent a flash of fear across Mama's face, and it jolted Oscar, too. Three years ago, a massive forest fire had erupted in the woods north of Castle. It burned thousands of acres of pine and birch trees, and then raced across the prairie toward Castle. Dozens of buildings were burned, including Oscar's barn. The entire town could have been lost. But just as flames were lapping at the edges of Main Street, a big rainstorm blew in and doused the fire.

"Don't worry," Mr. Morrow said, giving Mama a reassuring pat. "Chicago has one of the best fire departments in the country. We have close to two hundred firemen and a fleet of the best new steam pumpers. That fire will be out before we finish supper."

The cab lurched to a stop, and Joseph turned around. "And here we are, folks. Palmer House hotel. Finest in the city."

They climbed out of the cab, and a man in a top hat swung open the hotel's huge front door. Oscar peered inside at the glittering lobby. Bright lights twinkled, and piano music filled the air. Oscar lingered outside. He'd never seen such a fancy place, and he was sure he didn't belong in there.

Oscar glanced back at the street, tempted to bolt away to the train station.

And that's when he saw her — a little girl scurrying down the sidewalk. Even in the flickering gaslight, there was no mistaking that dirty yellow cap, those raggedy braids.

"There she is!" Oscar called out.

But Mama and Mr. Morrow were already starting across the lobby, and Oscar's shouts were drowned out by the music and the hum of the chattering crowd. The girl moved quickly across the sidewalk.

And before he even realized what he was doing, Oscar had dashed into the street.

He had to catch that little thief!

CHAPTER 5

10:15 P.M.
HEADING TOWARD THE SOUTH SIDE

Oscar dodged a speeding horse wagon and leaped over a steaming pile of manure. He hopped up onto the wooden sidewalk and wove his way through the crowd, his eyes glued to the yellow cap bobbing in front of him.

The girl didn't look like much of a criminal, with her stick legs and flapping braids. But wasn't that innocent look part of her act? Papa always said that Earless was a charmer. "He'll dazzle you with his smile then shoot you dead," Papa would say. Plus, Papa explained, Earless treated the guys in his gang like brothers. "He made sure they ate and drank like kings."

Oscar figured the girl was heading for the gang's hideout. His best bet was to secretly follow her there.

Oscar stayed hidden as he followed her through the busy streets. They crossed behind a tavern and then cut through a snaking alley. They finally came out onto a dark street of small houses and shacks. The girl beelined for a sagging little house set back from the street. Oscar ducked behind a barrel and waited as she used a key to open the front door.

"Bruno," she called out as she went inside. "I'm back!"

Bruno.

Must be one of the thugs, Oscar thought. He saw a piece of jagged wood lying on the ground. He grabbed it. It would make a decent weapon, just in case.

He crept up to the house, crouching low so none of the criminals would spot him out the window. He wondered what he should do. Barge in? Demand his suitcases? Suddenly his knees started to shake. Sweat oozed down his neck.

What was he doing? He needed to get out of here!

But then he thought of Papa facing the gun barrel of Earless Max Kildair. No, Oscar thought, he wasn't going to run scared from a bunch of street thugs. He was going to get Papa's badge back.

He curled his fingers around his weapon as he rose up, ready for a fight.

Oscar peered through the window.

He spotted the little thief.

And his mouth dropped open in shock.

No, he thought. *It can't be.*

He had imagined her sitting there with Otis Webber and the other boys, rummaging through piles of loot.

He'd gotten it wrong.

There were no thugs, and no sign of his suitcases.

The girl sat in a little wooden chair. On her lap was not a pile of stolen money and jewels but a smiling little boy with a mop of dark curls. Oscar guessed he was maybe three years old.

Their voices floated through the open window.

"Sorry I had to leave you alone again," she said.

"I very brave, Jennie," the boy said, puffing out his chest. His little croaking voice made Oscar think of the baby frogs he used to catch behind his house. "Next time I help."

"No," the girl said. "It's no fun, what I do. And you need to stay here and guard our house!"

The boy puffed out his chest proudly. "I guard."

"And guess what. I have enough money to get us some nice, fresh milk tomorrow."

"And a cookie?" the boy asked hopefully.

"We'll see," she said, taking off her yellow cap. She suddenly looked older than Oscar had first thought, maybe nine or ten. The boy reached up and tenderly smoothed one of the girl's crooked braids.

"I love cookies, Jennie," the boy whispered.

"I know you do, Brunie," Jennie said.

She smiled. But it was a weary kind of smile, tinged with sadness. It reminded Oscar of Mama's smile, how she looked in the months before Mr. Morrow appeared.

Oscar swallowed hard as he stepped away from the window. Those kids were on their own. Oscar felt it in his bones. He remembered what the policeman said: Otis Webber preyed on the most helpless orphans.

Oscar dropped his stupid weapon and headed slowly toward the road. What a dope he was, pretending he was like Papa, chasing a killer outlaw through Chicago.

Instead he'd found two sad little kids.

And now all he could think of was Mama.

How could he have left her like that?

She must be going crazy with worry.

His mind was so jumbled up that he barely noticed when something landed on top of his head. It felt like a leaf, or a big moth. He absent-mindedly brushed it away, then was startled when a shower of sparks spilled down in front of his face. A few hit his skin, burning his flesh like red-hot needles.

Oscar looked up and saw a sight so strange he was sure his eyes were playing tricks. It looked as if glowing red snowflakes were falling from the sky. They danced in the gusting wind, hundreds of hot, burning embers of different sizes and shapes. Before he knew what was happening, they were all around him, attacking like a swarm of fiery bees. They seared his scalp, burned through the wool of his clothes, scorched his lips. Pain lashed him, and the sickening smell of his burning hair made him gag.

And suddenly, *Whoosh!*

Flames leaped up in front of Oscar's face. The sparks had ignited his clothes.

Oscar was on fire!

CHAPTER 6

Oscar threw himself to the ground and rolled in the dirt, frantically beating the flames that were crawling up his arms and reaching out to grab his face. He rolled and pounded until finally the burning stopped. He lay there, coughing and spitting out the ashes that coated his tongue. His heart hammered with fear. But he couldn't just lie there. The sparks were still everywhere. He had to find somewhere to hide.

Gritting his teeth in pain, he managed to crawl back to an old chicken coop behind the kids' house. The wood was mostly rotted away, but the roof was just wide enough to protect Oscar. He sat hugging his knees to his chest, swatting away the sparks that came too close. He breathed deep, trying to slow his hammering heart.

He touched his forehead, gently rubbing his fingertips over the blistered skin. His scalp was badly singed, and there were burns up and down his body.

But he barely felt the throbbing pain. His attention was focused on the sky. That glow Mama had noticed earlier was brighter now. It

looked as though a giant hand had painted the sky bright orange.

The fire had gotten bigger.

Much bigger.

That's where the sparks and embers were coming from. The powerful wind was scattering them like burning dandelion seeds.

The same thing had happened the night of the forest fire near Castle. Sparks and hunks of burning wood and bark had flown for miles, setting off new fires wherever they landed. Mama and Papa and Oscar had almost lost their barn. Some people lost everything — barns, houses, even fields. Ten people were killed. One family survived by diving into their pond and dunking under the water while the flames roared over them.

Oscar took a breath, trying to loosen the choking fear that gripped his throat.

He thought of what Mr. Morrow had said — that Chicago had one of the best fire departments in America.

Maybe that was true, but there was no sign of them here.

And once a fire got too big, not even an army of firefighters could put it out. Oscar had learned for himself during the Castle fire how a fire could grow and grow, how it could become like a ferocious beast that would devour everything in its path. And what a fire was most hungry for was wood — like the thousands of shacks and stores that lined Chicago's streets, the miles of wooden sidewalks, the warehouses filled with coal and oil that would explode at the slightest spark.

Oscar remembered how the forest looked, after the fire. He and Papa had ridden up there to see it for themselves. Oscar would never forget the sight of it. The fire had turned thousands of trees into twisted black stubs. The ground was a sea of ash. There was not a bird, not an insect to be seen. Oscar had tried not to look at the blackened bones that were scattered all around, the skeletons of the creatures that hadn't been able to escape.

He and Papa had both loved that forest. They'd go up there with Mama, who loved telling them the names of every last tree and flower. Oscar and Papa had both fought back tears as they stood in the burned ruins. But then Papa had pointed to something on the ground — a tiny green shoot pushing up through the ash.

"It will take a long time," Papa had said. "But one day the forest will grow back."

Oscar shivered as he thought of what a huge fire like that could do to a city like Chicago.

Could such an important city burn to the ground?

It didn't seem possible.

But hadn't Oscar learned that anything was possible?

If a blizzard could kill his papa, couldn't a fire destroy an entire city?

Oscar looked up, as though answers might be printed on the orange sky.

But instead, his eyes found the two small and terrified faces peering down at him from the upstairs window of the house.

Jennie and Bruno.

The sight of them, lit up by the glowing sky, jolted him.

Right at that second, the wind blew its dragon breath. More sparks and embers appeared, and out of nowhere, a large plank of flaming wood came soaring through the air. It was like an enormous flaming spear, hurled by an invisible warrior.

It was heading right for the house!

Boom!

The wood smashed through the roof of the house, sending a column of flames high into the air.

Oscar opened his mouth, but he was too horrified to even scream.

CHAPTER 7

Oscar sprinted toward the house, swatting away the burning flakes that swarmed around him. He watched with terror as the fire quickly danced across the roof.

Where were the kids? Why hadn't they come bursting through the door?

"Come on, come on," he whispered, as though he could grab hold of them with his words.

But still they did not appear.

Oscar rushed up the crumbling steps and pounded on the front door.

"Hey!" he shouted. "Come out!"

Nothing. He tried the door, but it was locked tight.

Where were they?

Shouts rang out from the street.

"Fire! Fire! Fire!"

Oscar whirled around.

Two other houses were burning like torches. The wind gusted, and flames leaped across the street.

Boom!

The house caught fire as if it were made of dried straw.

Any minute this whole street would be a sea of fire. Oscar had to get away!

He had to get back to Mama!

But how could he leave here if those kids were still in the house?

Of course he couldn't. Oscar slammed his shoulder into the door.

Bam!

Bam!

Bam!

On the third try the door frame splintered, and the door burst open. Oscar stumbled in, falling to his knees. Smoke swirled all around him. He rose to his feet, gasping for breath.

"Hello!" he screamed. "Where are you?"

And that's when he heard them, just above the fire's roar, muffled cries coming from upstairs. Or was it just the wind and the fire fooling his ears?

Was it possible the kids had escaped through another door?

Oscar stumbled to the narrow staircase, peering up into a churning cloud of black smoke.

Don't be an idiot, he told himself. *Don't go up those stairs!*

"Hello!" Oscar called, praying that nobody would answer, that the kids were long gone.

But no.

"Help us! Please!" shouted a terrified voice, the girl's.

There was no choice.

On shaking legs, Oscar started up the stairs. He pulled his shirt up over his mouth and nose. It did nothing to block out the smoke. Each breath burned his throat and lungs. But the worst was the blistering heat. With each step, it grew hotter.

Oscar could practically feel his blood boiling, his skin sizzling, his flesh cooking on his bones.

He wouldn't last long up here. And neither would Jennie and Bruno.

At the top of the stairs was a closed door. Someone pounded on the other side.

"Here!" Jennie shouted. "The door is stuck! Please help us!"

Oscar pushed against the door, but it wouldn't budge.

"Stand back!" he choked.

Oscar kicked the door as hard as he could.

The door crashed open, releasing a wave of heat and even thicker smoke that pushed Oscar back on his heels. He teetered and almost fell down the stairs. But somehow he managed to regain his balance. Jennie came rushing out with Bruno in her arms. They were both coughing and wheezing. Their faces were black with soot and streaked with tears.

Jennie was clutching Bruno with all her might, but her skinny arms were losing their grip.

Oscar reached for Bruno, and to his surprise the kid didn't resist. Oscar pulled Bruno into his arms, holding him close to his chest. The poor boy's heart was pounding even harder than Oscar's. Jennie stood unmoving, dazed, and coughing. Oscar was afraid she might faint.

Oscar grabbed her arm and pointed her down the stairs, gripping her shoulder in case she slipped. He followed right on her heels.

"Run straight through the front door!" Oscar said to her. "Go as quickly as you can!"

Jennie did what she was told, gaining strength as they reached the bottom.

Oscar put Bruno down at the bottom of the stairs, and Jennie grabbed the little boy's hand. Together they flew out the door. Oscar was just steps behind them.

And then —

Crash!

The window shattered.

KABOOM!

A giant ball of fire and cinders blasted into the room.

Oscar fell to the floor.

And then there was nothing but flames.

CHAPTER 8

Again, Oscar felt as though he were being attacked by a wild animal, a monster with burning tentacles and boiling breath. It grabbed him, clawed at him, and spun him around.

Smoke gushed into his nose and down his throat, filling his lungs with searing poison. His couldn't open his eyes, but he knew the fire was all around him. He dropped to the ground, crawling blindly, groping for the door.

But he had no idea where he was. It was like being trapped in a flaming maze.

His lungs were ready to explode.

Was this the end? Was he really going to die right here?

And then he heard a voice.

"This way! This way!"

Mama?

"Turn right! Turn right!" the voice shouted, tugging him, guiding him.

Oscar turned.

No, it wasn't Mama's voice.

It was Jennie's.

"Yes! Now straight! Hurry!"

And then he felt a hand on his arm, pulling him up.

Seconds later he was out the door.

He was just steps away from the house when there was a terrifying *whoosh* and an explosion of hot air.

They rushed forward, and Jennie grabbed Bruno from where he had been hiding behind a barrel. They ran across the street and fell to the ground.

Oscar's head throbbed; his entire body felt as if it had been roasted.

He lay back and closed his eyes.

For a long minute, he stayed there, trying to catch his breath.

He might have stayed like that for hours. But only a minute or so passed before he felt someone breathing in his face.

He opened his eyes and saw a huge curly head hovering over him with wide-open eyes.

Bruno.

"Hey! You not dead!" he croaked out happily.

"Hush, Bruno!" Jennie whispered. "That is not a polite thing to say!"

"But he not dead!" Bruno insisted, putting his face even closer to Oscar's, so his slimy little nose touched Oscar's nose. Then he put his gooey mouth to Oscar's ear and whispered, "You not dead."

The kid wasn't going to quit.

Oscar put his hand on Bruno's head.

"I know," he said.

Jennie kneeled down and gently peeled Bruno away from Oscar.

"Let's give him a little room," Jennie said.

Oscar managed to sit up.

He stared ahead at the little house, which was being torn apart by the flames. The wood moaned and sighed as it collapsed into the fire, as if crying out in pain. It was sickening, like watching a rabbit get torn apart by a coyote.

Bruno wriggled closer to Oscar until his small shoulder pressed against Oscar's arm.

"My house," he said, pointing sadly.

Oscar didn't know what to say, so he just put an arm around the boy.

The fire burned so bright that it lit up all their faces.

It was the first time Jennie had the chance to get a good look at Oscar. Now Oscar waited to see the shock in her eyes when she realized who he was.

But there was no flash of recognition. She looked exactly how Oscar felt: scared, dazed, and amazed to be alive.

Their eyes locked together, and Oscar could tell that Jennie didn't recognize the kid she'd tricked at the train station. She saw a different boy, the boy who'd helped her and Bruno escape from the fire.

And as Oscar looked at Jennie, he didn't see a helpless orphan or a ruthless thief. He saw a brave girl who watched over her brother all by herself, whose voice had led Oscar out of the blazing house in the nick of time.

And then there was Bruno, who grinned at Oscar as though they'd been best friends all their lives.

"I Boono," he said, looking up at Oscar and puffing out his chest.

"I'm Oscar," Oscar said.

"Occar," Bruno said.

"I'm Jennie," Jennie said.

They all sat there a minute, looking at each other. Had he and Jennie really only just laid eyes on each other tonight?

Oscar eased his arm from around Bruno and struggled to his feet, brushing the dust and ashes off his burned clothes.

His body ached, but his mind felt surprisingly clear. He knew exactly what to do.

"We need to get to the Palmer House hotel," he said.

He said the word *we* very clearly.

"My mother is there," Oscar said. "The hotel is fireproof. We'll be safe there."

Oscar picked up Bruno and held out his free hand to Jennie.

She took it, and gripped it tight.

And together they began their journey through Chicago's burning streets.

CHAPTER 9

MONDAY, OCTOBER 9
12:15 A.M.
THE SOUTH SIDE OF CHICAGO,
HEADING NORTH

They left Jennie and Bruno's burning neighborhood behind and headed north. Oscar kept looking over his shoulder at that giant orange glow bleeding through the sky. The main fire was huge now, Oscar could see, and it was spreading fast.

And the wind was carrying sparks all over the

city. Everywhere Oscar looked, he saw new fires burning.

Some fires were very small — a ribbon of flame waving from a tree, a pile of garbage glowing like a campfire.

But there were burning houses everywhere, and in places, the smoke was so thick that they had to gasp for breath.

But Oscar's gasps also came from what was happening all around them: people sobbing and screaming, horses driven crazy by the heat and sparks, stray dogs howling in fear. Even the rats were running for their lives, rushing out from under the wooden sidewalks and getting squashed under the wheels of the wagons and buggies that plowed through the streets.

The crowds got bigger as they moved north. Many people were dragging trunks and suitcases, or struggling with heavy sacks heaved over their shoulders. Two women in nightgowns carried a mattress above their heads. On top was a very old man, curled up under a quilt.

The fires turned the night as bright as day, lighting up the terrified faces all around Oscar — the tearstained cheeks, the mouths open in horror, the wide-open eyes looking up at the sky.

But the worst part was the howling wind, which seemed to be getting stronger by the minute. Each hot gust was filled with dust and smoke, and spit out millions of embers and sparks. One burned a hole clear through the toe of Oscar's boot. Oscar passed a woman just as her skirts erupted into flames. Luckily the man next to her had a canteen of water, and quickly drenched her.

The sparks were terrible for Oscar and Jennie, but they tortured poor Bruno.

"Hot! Hot!" he kept saying, trying to bury his face in Oscar's neck.

Finally Jennie spotted an overturned wheelbarrow with a heap of clothes spilling out. She snatched a lady's hat, its purple velvet smudged with dirt, the wide brim crushed.

"I don't think anyone will miss this," she said.

She put it on Bruno's head, a perfect helmet to protect his curls. She kept her eyes on Oscar, swatting away embers that came too close to his face or smoldered on his clothes.

Oscar was getting the idea that there wasn't much Jennie couldn't take care of.

They came to a corner where a crowd of people had stopped to watch a grand brick building burn. Oscar and Jennie tried to push their way through, but they were completely hemmed in.

And then, suddenly, the clanging of bells rose above the roar of the fire.

"Fire department!" someone shouted.

People jumped out of the way as two steam pumper wagons came tearing around the corner, each pulled by two sweating horses. A hose wagon followed.

Oscar's heart lifted a bit.

He remembered what Mr. Morrow had told them, that Chicago had the best fire department in the world. And here was their chance to prove it. Maybe they could save at least part of the city.

People in the crowd watched hopefully as about fifteen firefighters hopped off the wagons and got to work, readying the pumper and

uncoiling the heavy canvas hoses. In Castle, there was no fire department or pumper engines. When a fire broke out, people had to rely on themselves and their neighbors. During the big fire, a flurry of sparks had ignited the roof of Oscar's barn. Within minutes, thirty people had rushed to their farm, ready to help. They grabbed every bucket and jug they could find, and formed a bucket brigade.

Mama and two other women had stood at the well, filling the buckets as fast as they could. Everyone else lined up, forming a human chain that led from the well to the barn. Oscar stood on the line, passing sloshing buckets of cold water toward the fire. It was amazing how those heavy buckets flew across the chain of hands, how the splashes of water tamed the flames.

Oscar had kept going even after his arms were numb with pain.

It had taken an hour, but they'd put the fire out. The roof of the barn was burned through, but the rest of the building still stood.

Oscar would never forget how happy he felt when the last of the flames fizzled out, as if he'd helped slay a monster.

He watched now as the firefighters dragged the heavy coils over to the burning buildings, screaming at people in the crowd to stand back as the pumper engines roared and water pulsed into the hoses. Like soldiers in battle, the men aimed their hoses. Cheers rose up from the crowd as thick, powerful sprays of water blasted up at the flames.

Very quickly Oscar realized that the firefighters didn't stand a chance. The fire was too big and too hot. The water hissed as it got close to the flames, and then boiled away into puffs of steam. With every gust of wind, the flames rose higher, twisting and dancing in the sky as though teasing the firefighters.

They'd need an ocean to put out those flames, Oscar reckoned, or a bucket brigade of a thousand people.

"Come on," Jennie said, spotting a break in the crowd.

As they pushed their way through, Oscar turned to take a last look at the firefighters. There was no mistaking the fear on their faces.

There was no doubt: Chicago was doomed.

CHAPTER 10

The three of them walked for at least an hour more, inching their way along the packed sidewalks. They were getting closer to the Palmer House, Jennie said. But new fires kept forcing them to find alternate routes.

Now they were caught in a sea of hundreds of bodies. People squeezed them on all sides, and Oscar struggled to stay on his feet.

They were passing by a warehouse when suddenly —

KABOOM!

The smell of oil filled the air, and shards of wood flew all around them.

"Run!" someone screamed.

Boom! Boom! Boom!

The explosions rang out like cannon fire.

Like a herd of cattle startled by a clap of thunder, the crowd erupted into a stampede. Oscar, Jennie, and Bruno were caught right in the middle. Elbows jabbed them, boots mashed Oscar's feet.

He watched as parents were torn away from their children. A woman fell and didn't get up again.

"Hold on tight, Bruno!" Oscar ordered, locking his arm around the boy as he gripped Jennie's hand so hard he was sure he would crush it.

If they were separated now, they'd never find each other again.

Luckily the street widened slightly, and they managed to burst out of the crushing crowd.

Jennie led them down a side street, and finally into a wide alley.

"State Street is just a block away from here,"

Jennie said as they caught their breath. "The Palmer House will be right there."

Halfway down the alley, they discovered a water barrel. They all ran toward it, desperate to quench their thirst and to cool their burning skin. Oscar felt like a stalk of wheat, shriveled in the boiling sun.

He hoisted the lid off and held Bruno while the boy slurped up water like a thirsty horse.

When he was finally done, Oscar and Jennie took turns, scooping up handfuls of the cool water and gulping them down. They splashed

the soothing water on their faces and down scorched necks and arms.

Oscar sighed with relief.

"You really know your way around the city," he said to Jennie as he dabbed drops of water onto his burned forehead. "You'd make a good tracker."

"My mother was a baker," Jennie said, with a hint of pride. "Bruno and I used to go with her to deliver her cakes and cookies."

"I love cookies," Bruno whispered to Oscar, as though he was sharing a deep secret.

A picture popped into Oscar's mind. He saw Jennie with her braids straight and glossy, Bruno nibbling on a cookie almost as big as his head. He pictured a lady with Bruno's dark curls and Jennie's big brown eyes, standing in the kitchen in a flowered apron.

"My mama got sick," Bruno said softly. "She in heaven."

Jennie glanced at Oscar and he glimpsed the fresh hurt in her eyes.

"My papa's in heaven, too," Oscar said, swallowing the lump in his throat.

"Our father died right after Bruno was born, in an accident," Jennie said. "Mama died six months ago. I promised her I'd keep an eye on Bruno, no matter what."

Oscar thought of his own promise to Papa: to watch over the farm. That promise had kept him going these past two years. But now it was broken.

Would Papa forgive him? Would Oscar forgive himself?

Jennie put her hand on Bruno's head.

"I couldn't let us go to the orphanage," Jennie said.

Her voice dropped very low when she said *orphanage*, as if it was a curse word no one should ever say.

Oscar understood.

He'd heard horror stories about the orphanage in Minneapolis, the city closest to Castle — that it was more like a jail than a home.

Oscar looked at Jennie and Bruno, suddenly wondering what would happen to them. Their home was gone. They were all alone.

What would they do?

But no, Oscar suddenly remembered. They weren't alone.

He picked up Bruno.

They weren't alone because they had Oscar.

"Hey, Bruno," he said. "I bet up in heaven, my papa and your parents are good friends."

Bruno leaned back so he could look Oscar in the eye.

"Like us!" he exclaimed.

His soot-covered face grinned out from under the fancy lady's hat.

Both Oscar and Jennie laughed, and for that second Oscar forgot about the smoke and the flames.

But their smiles didn't last long.

They'd just started walking through the alley again when they heard loud voices. A group of boys swung into the alley from the street. They were walking toward them.

Jennie froze.

Then Oscar saw who they were: the boys from the train station. And there, right in front, with his rattlesnake eyes glowing through the smoke, was Otis Webber.

CHAPTER 11

Otis had four other boys with him, each of them lugging a large sack. Otis was carrying a painting in a fancy gold frame. Oscar immediately understood: Otis and his gang had been looting — stealing from houses whose owners had fled the fire.

Oscar pulled Jennie closer to him and held Bruno tight.

Maybe the boys would just walk by, Oscar told himself. Maybe they were too busy with their stolen treasures to even notice them.

But Otis was the type who didn't miss a thing.

His yellow-tinged eyes scanned the alley and then landed right on Jennie.

He stopped short, and the other boys nearly knocked into him.

"Jennie," he said.

He sounded almost friendly.

Oscar studied him. The other boys looked around the same age, maybe fourteen or fifteen, and two were bigger than Otis. But Otis was the leader, without a doubt.

For a second, Oscar wondered if Otis wasn't so bad. Sure, he was a crook. But maybe Otis was good to the kids in his gang. Didn't Papa say that Earless treated the guys in his gang like brothers?

But Oscar saw that Jennie's hands were shaking.

"Hi, Otis," she said softly.

"Glad we found you," he said. "We need more hands. It's a big night for us! We won't have to work again for a year."

Jennie kept her eyes on the ground.

"So come on," he said. "Leave the baby with your buddy here."

"I not baby," Bruno growled.

At least one person here wasn't terrified of Otis. Otis smiled.

"Tough kid," he said, spitting on the ground. "We'll take him along, too."

"No!" Jennie said, her face suddenly fierce.

Otis raised his eyebrows.

"I quit," she said.

"You quit?" Otis laughed, a strange high-pitched giggle that raised the hairs on Oscar's neck. He looked around at the other boys, who laughed nervously.

But then his face went dead.

"No one quits my gang," he said in a low voice. "You know that. That's how it works."

Anger rose up in Oscar as he imagined how Otis had gotten all these kids to work for him, how he picked the ones whose parents were gone, who were starving and desperate to stay out of orphanages.

How helpless Jennie must have been when her mother died! She was willing to do anything to keep herself and Bruno out of the orphanage — even work for that snake.

"Leave her alone," Oscar said, louder than he'd meant to.

And now Otis turned his menacing stare on Oscar. For the first time, he realized he'd seen Oscar before. He smiled chillingly.

"You!" he said. "You looking for your suit-cases? You think Jennie's gonna get them back for you?"

Jennie looked at Oscar in confusion, but then her face seemed to crumble.

Otis put the painting down and lunged toward Jennie.

"No!" Oscar cried.

And before he realized what he was doing, he sprang forward and gave Otis a hard push in the chest.

The thug stumbled back, stomping on the painting.

Snap!

It broke in half.

Time seemed to stop.

The four boys behind Otis backed up, as if they were afraid Otis might explode.

And he did.

Otis reached into his jacket and pulled out a huge knife.

Jennie staggered back, and Bruno went running into her arms.

But it wasn't Jennie whom Otis came at with the knife. It was Oscar.

Otis sprang forward and placed the blade against Oscar's cheek.

Oscar closed his eyes, bracing himself for the slicing metal.

But it was Otis's other hand that came swinging up.

Smack!

His rocklike fist smashed into Oscar's nose.

Oscar fell to the ground, the flash of pain in his head burning brighter than the blazing sky.

CHAPTER 12

Oscar had no idea how long he lay in the alley, dead to the world.

When the blackness started to lift from his mind, all he could feel was pain. His nose seemed crushed, his brain knocked loose.

Where was he?

All he knew was that something terrible had happened to him.

Had he been kicked by one of the horses? Had he fallen from the roof of the barn?

He smelled smoke. Was the prairie on fire again?

And where was Mama?

But then pictures flashed through his throbbing skull — glittering yellow eyes, the flash of a knife blade, a little girl with raggedy braids.

And then his eyelids shot open.

Jennie! Bruno!

He sat up and looked around, fighting back tears.

They were gone.

Otis Webber had taken both of them.

Oscar struggled to breathe.

And now it was his panic, and not the smoke, that choked his lungs.

He struggled to stand up, wobbling as he found his balance.

"Jennie!" he cried. "Bruno!" The words came out as a rasping whisper.

But he called their names again and again as he staggered down the alley, past the water barrel, and back out into the street.

On the street were dozens of people fleeing north, pushing their carts and wheelbarrows and hauling their sacks. The sparks and embers rained down. Nobody noticed the boy with the blood-smeared face and swollen eyes, frantically searching the crowd.

Part of Oscar wanted to go back into the alley, to curl up. Maybe the wind would sweep him up and carry him back to Castle — to anywhere but here.

But even in his dazed and muddled state, he knew he would not do that. He had to get to the Palmer House, to find Mama.

And Mr. Morrow.

If anyone could find Jennie and Bruno, it was Mr. Morrow.

He remembered that Jennie said they were just one block away from the hotel.

He ran back into the alley and then cut through a side street one block.

He came out on a wide avenue.

And there it was, the Palmer House hotel.

The massive building was in flames. The roof had caved in, and piles of crumbled marble and wood lay in heaps in the street.

The fire must have been burning for hours.

Mama and Mr. Morrow couldn't possibly still be here.

Fire gushed out of the hotel's windows. Black smoke churned through the roof. But it wasn't the sight of the burning Palmer House that turned Oscar's insides to jelly.

It was what he saw when he turned and looked up the street.

It was a gigantic wave of fire. It was wider than the street, with flames towering hundreds of feet into the air.

It looked like the sun had burst open, and its fiery blood was gushing onto the city.

Oscar understood what was happening, because the same had happened during the Castle fire. Smaller fires joined together into one monstrous blaze. Oscar and Mama had heard the terrifying stories from people who had witnessed the fire up close — and barely escaped with their lives. They described a fire so big that it seemed to stretch forever across the prairie, and so high it seemed to be trying to roast the moon. It raced across the prairie, faster than a horse could gallop. One man swore that a tornado of fire appeared out of nowhere and lifted his house off the ground.

These stories haunted Oscar for months. He'd wake up at night soaked in sweat, convinced his house was burning. Walking home from school, he'd keep eyes peeled and aimed at the sky, convinced that a flaming twister was going to carry him away.

And now those nightmares were coming true.

The wall of fire roared down the street, devouring everything in its path. The wind gusted, a hot and poisonous blast that almost knocked Oscar off his feet. Oscar watched in horror as a blazing sheet peeled off the fire. It swirled through the air, a flaming twister bigger and more horrifying than anything Oscar could have imagined. It flew down the street, hundreds of yards.

BOOM!

It exploded into a tall building, igniting it.

Now the street was blocked on both sides, with the flames spreading fast.

Oscar stood there, frozen in fear.

He had no idea what to do, where to go.

But then he heard someone calling his name.

"Oscar!"

It rose up above the fire's lion roar, like a kindly giant calling from his castle in the sky.

Oscar whirled around.

A shadow appeared through the cloud of smoke.

He saw a familiar face, and he let himself fall into the strong arms that reached out for him.

It was Mr. Morrow.

CHAPTER 13

"Your mother is safe at my house!" Mr. Morrow shouted over the roaring fire.

One of Mr. Morrow's friends had taken Mama there in a buggy, hours before.

"My house is far to the north," he said. "The flames won't reach there. She didn't want to leave the hotel. But I promised her that I would find you."

He explained this as they ran to the corner. The streets were practically deserted; almost everyone else on the block had already fled.

Mr. Morrow had stayed behind, risking his life to look for Oscar.

Oscar opened his mouth to thank him, to tell him about Jennie and Bruno.

But his voice was wrecked from the smoke and his shouting. And he didn't know how to begin. A cab stood at the corner, the horse covered with a soaking-wet blanket to protect it from the sparks.

A familiar voice shouted to them through the smoke. "Got him, Charlie?"

It was Joseph, the cabdriver Oscar had met earlier.

"I do!" Mr. Morrow called.

"Mr. Morrow's got half the city of Chicago looking for you, son," Joseph said as they climbed in.

Seconds later they were inside the buggy, and the horse took off in a gallop.

The two walls of flame were moving toward each other, but Joseph steered his horse through the middle and then swerved onto a side street that the fire hadn't yet touched.

Most horses would have refused to budge in a

fire like this, or would be rearing up in wild panic. But the old nag was calm, and Joseph barely had to snap the reins to keep her moving quickly.

"Joseph is taking us to the nearest bridge," Mr. Morrow said. "We'll cross the river there and make our way to my house. There are fires on the other side, but nothing like this."

Mr. Morrow shook his head.

"I can't believe it, Oscar," he said. "So much is gone."

The courthouse was in ruins, Mr. Morrow said. So were the new opera house, the grand department stores, and the huge factories and train depots. Thousands of houses were gone.

"I don't know what will be left when this is all over," Mr. Morrow said.

The bridge came into view. It was wide, with a roadway in the center and two narrow walkways on either side.

Oscar's heart sank as he saw the hundreds of people knotted together on the bridge, the dozens of buggies creeping along.

"Charlie," Joseph said. "You're better off on foot. And I need to get up to my sister's house, to check on her."

"Of course," Mr. Morrow said.

He and Oscar climbed out, and Mr. Morrow reached up to shake hands with Joseph.

"Thanks. I'll see you, friend," Mr. Morrow said.

"You sure will," Joseph said.

But Oscar could see the doubt in both men's eyes.

They were standing in front of a paint warehouse, and Mr. Morrow looked at the bridge. His face was etched with worry.

"I don't like the look of that bridge," he said. "The roadway is made of wood. It could burn at any time. If the fire comes, all of those people will be trapped. It will be complete panic."

Oscar remembered the horror of being stuck in the stampeding crowd with Jennie and Bruno. He knew Mr. Morrow was right, that the bridge was unsafe. But how else could they get across the river?

He looked out on the water. Farther up were boats steaming and sailing in both directions. But this stretch was mostly empty.

"There," Mr. Morrow said, spotting a rowboat tied up along the riverbank. "I used to row across all the time when I was a kid. It takes just a few minutes."

They hurried to the boat.

"Climb in," Mr. Morrow said. "I'm going to see if I can find another set of oars."

It was only when Oscar got into the boat that he realized his whole body was shaking. But the thought of seeing Mama made him feel stronger.

"Here," Mr. Morrow said, handing Oscar a set of oars. "We're going to have to move very quickly."

Soon they had shoved off and were rowing with all their might.

Oil fumes rose up, and something worse — that slaughterhouse stench. Garbage and dead rats floated around them. With so many factories lining the shores, Oscar knew the water must be a filthy witch's brew.

The wind blew hard, sending showers of sparks over the river.

Shouts and screams rang out from the bridge. Oscar saw that a wagon in the middle of the bridge roadway had caught fire.

Oscar closed his eyes and tried to block out the screams.

Next came splashes, and Oscar refused to think about what — or who — was falling off the bridge and into the river.

He looked in the other direction and gasped in horror.

A large sailboat was racing through the water. The mast was burning. There was nobody at the helm. It looked like a ghost ship, evil and glowing.

And it was heading right for them.

CHAPTER 14

"Row faster, Oscar!" Mr. Morrow shouted.

But the flaming boat was too big and moving too quickly for them to get out of the way in time.

"Oscar!" Mr. Morrow said. "Can you swim?"

"Yes," Oscar said.

"Good," he said. "Swim to shore. When you get to the other side, get yourself to the lakeshore."

Why was Mr. Morrow telling him this?

There was no time to ask.

The burning ship was closing in.

"Jump!" Mr. Morrow cried.

Oscar threw himself over the side. The cold water slapped him and burned his skin. He started swimming as fast as he could, keeping his eyes and mouth closed against the foul water.

Crash!

Sparks flew up all around as the flaming ship hit the rowboat, slicing it in half and setting it on fire.

Oscar kept swimming. He glanced over his shoulder, expecting to see Mr. Morrow right beside him.

But he wasn't.

Oscar stopped and turned, churning his legs and arms to stay afloat.

Through the smoke, he saw something bobbing in the water.

It was Mr. Morrow clinging to a small piece of wood and struggling to keep his head above water.

Now Oscar understood why Mr. Morrow didn't think he could make it to the other side of the river. He couldn't swim!

Oscar should have known — Papa couldn't swim either, even though he grew up near the ocean. Mama was one of the few people Oscar knew who could swim, and it was she who had taught Oscar.

"Keep going, Oscar!" Mr. Morrow cried.

Oscar saw a huge piece of wood floating near him. He grabbed it and kicked as hard as he could to get to Mr. Morrow.

"Mr. Morrow! Grab hold."

Mr. Morrow looked up in surprise and relief as Oscar thrust the wood toward him.

And that's when Oscar noticed that back on the south shore, from where they'd just escaped, the roof of the paint warehouse had caught fire.

His heart leaped into his throat. Any minute, there would be a massive explosion.

They had to get away now!

They both clung to the makeshift raft, kicking frantically.

And then —

KABOOM!

Behind them, the paint factory exploded with a deafening blast.

Oscar waited for the crush of burning wood, for flames to reach out and grab them.

But instead, the force of the explosion created a wave that came up behind them. It propelled them forward, out of the fire's reach, toward the safety of the north shore.

They landed with a thud on the muddy riverbank. Oscar looked back, amazed to see that the river itself was now on fire.

He could barely believe they'd made it. Yet he felt little relief.

Oscar stared over the flaming river. The entire south side of the city was in the grip of fire and smoke. And somewhere in the middle of it all were Jennie and Bruno.

Oscar told Mr. Morrow all about them as they trudged away from the river. Mr. Morrow listened closely, and Oscar sensed that he was using Oscar's words to paint a picture of Bruno and Jennie in his mind.

"We'll find them, Oscar," he kept saying. "I found you, didn't I?"

But the search for Jennie and Bruno would have to wait. Because once again Oscar and Mr. Morrow found themselves in a fight for their lives. They kept trying to get back to Mr. Morrow's house, but the wind grew stronger and stronger, sweeping ferocious fires all through the north side of the river. Entire blocks burned within minutes. Flames chased after Oscar and Mr. Morrow. Each time they thought they were safe, a new fire would erupt, and they were on the run again.

Their last hope was Lake Michigan, which stretched out to the east of the city.

As the fires closed in behind them, they waded into the freezing water, ready to duck under if the flames attacked. There were hundreds of people all around them, and the crowd grew to the thousands as the night wore on.

There were entire families with their horses and with their wagons piled high with furniture, fancy ladies in their ruffled dresses and jewels, children who had been separated from their parents. They all stood gasping in the smoky air, shivering in the freezing water.

The hours crept by, the sun came up, and still the fires raged out of control. It would be another endless day before finally the fires began to tire, when the winds lost their fury, when it was finally safe enough to wade out of the freezing water.

It took hours more for Oscar and Mr. Morrow to make their way back to his house in the pouring rain. They were numb with cold and shock, miserable with thirst, and wheezing in the smoky air.

But finally they made it to Mr. Morrow's stone house, one of the few houses still standing. And there, on the porch, was Mama. Oscar got the idea that she'd been standing there for days.

She sprinted off the porch and into the drenching rain to meet them.

Her face was as pale as bone.

Oscar ran to her, throwing himself into her arms.

They fell to their knees, their tears mixing with the raindrops that put out the last flickering flames of Chicago's fire.

CHAPTER 15

EIGHT DAYS LATER
OCTOBER 18, 5:30 P.M.
MR. MORROW'S HOUSE,
BELDEN AVENUE, CHICAGO

The day was bright and clear. Oscar stood in Mr. Morrow's studio.

Mr. Morrow had been right — this was Oscar's favorite room in the house. He liked the view of the lake in the distance.

But best of all were Mr. Morrow's paintings that lined the walls and crowded the shelves.

Oscar's favorites, of course, were four paintings that Mr. Morrow had created of their farm in Castle. Oscar came up here every day to look at them.

Voices drifted from the kitchen, along with the scent of baking cookies. Oscar breathed deep, wanting to take in the sweet smells. Finally he could take a breath without doubling over into a coughing fit. His lungs were healing, now, his burns and cuts scabbing over. But he couldn't shake the nightmares that haunted him every night. It was always the same, how he'd wake up shouting two words over and over:

"Jennie! Bruno!"

Oscar would sit in bed, his heart hammering, tears streaming down his cheeks, as he thought of them lost and alone in the burning city.

The search for Jennie and Bruno had started the morning after Oscar and Mr. Morrow got back to the house. Dozens of Mr. Morrow's friends helped them. They scoured the lakefront, where thousands of people were living in makeshift tents. They searched Lincoln Park, which was packed with thousands more.

Day after day they all searched, but there was no sign of Jennie and Bruno. And there were moments when Oscar feared the worst.

"Have hope," Mr. Morrow kept saying.

But it was hard to have hope when all Oscar could see in any direction was smoldering ruins. Hundreds of people were dead, and four miles of the city had burned to the ground.

As they walked through the streets, Mr. Morrow kept his arm around Oscar's shoulders. He'd point to men carting away wagonloads of wreckage, at the new shacks popping up on still-smoldering lots.

Mr. Morrow reminded Oscar of Papa, that day in the ruined forest. Just as Papa had seen those little green shoots popping through the ash, Mr. Morrow already saw signs that Chicago would be rebuilt.

And then Mr. Morrow had the idea of drawing Jennie and Bruno's picture and having it printed in the newspaper. Oscar described their faces, and Mr. Morrow's pencil brought them to life. The picture was printed in the *Chicago Tribune*, along with an ad:

Mr. Charles Morrow and the Chicago police seek information about two missing children, Jennie, approximately 9, and Bruno, approximately 3.

Oscar had insisted that Mr. Morrow add one more detail to the picture: the battered purple lady's hat on Bruno's head.

The very next day, the police received a tip from a woman on the city's west side, in a neighborhood that hadn't been burned. The woman had always been suspicious of one of her neighbors. The man lived alone, but rough-looking boys were always showing up at odd hours, often carrying large sacks and suitcases through the back door of the house.

The woman was reading the newspaper, and Mr. Morrow's drawing caught her eye. She'd seen two kids in front of the neighbor's house just that morning. She wouldn't have looked twice, except for something very strange about the boy — the purple lady's hat on his head.

Oscar had been up here in the studio, standing in this exact spot, when he'd heard the clatter of hooves outside. He'd looked out the window, and there was Joseph's cab, pulled by his faithful old nag. Oscar figured it was more of Mr. Morrow's friends coming to stay. Mr. Morrow and Mama kept the door wide open to anyone who needed a bed or a meal, and the house was overflowing.

Oscar had turned away from the window, but then he'd heard a croaking voice shouting up to him.

"Occar!"

He'd looked out the window and his heart just about burst apart — it was Jennie and Bruno. They were ragged and dusty but all in one piece. Oscar's knees momentarily went weak, and then he'd practically flown down the stairs.

Oscar had scooped Bruno up and held him tight. He grabbed Jennie's hand.

He could hardly believe it. He still couldn't. They were back together — for good now. Mama and Mr. Morrow made sure they all understood that.

Oscar had to wait until later that night, after Bruno was asleep, for Jennie to tell Oscar and Mama and Mr. Morrow the whole incredible story — how they'd escaped the fire, how Otis had brought them to the house of a man he obviously knew very well. It turned out this man was the gang's real leader.

"What was he like?" Mama asked.

"Believe it or not, he didn't act like a wicked criminal," Jennie said. "He gave us plenty to eat, and he had a very friendly smile."

But there was one thing about the man Jennie said she'd never forget.

"The man had only one ear."

Oscar and Mama had stared at each other in disbelief.

But it turned out to be true: The man was Earless Max Kildair.

And Papa had been right about the gangster still being up to no good.

Now Earless was in jail, where he belonged. Otis Webber and his gang had disappeared, but Jennie and Bruno wouldn't have to worry about them anymore.

The police recovered thousands of dollars of silver and paintings from Kildair's house. They also found three suitcases.

The baking smells were getting stronger, and Oscar heard pattering feet running up the stairs.

Bruno burst in, Papa's badge pinned to his puffed-out chest.

"Occar!" he cried. "Come on! They ready!"

Jennie was right behind him. Her new dress was speckled with flour; she loved helping Mama in the kitchen.

She and Oscar grinned at each other. Her face was bright now, her braids glossy and straight. But looking at her, Oscar knew he'd always see that same brave girl who'd led him through the flames.

Bruno pulled Oscar toward the door.

"Come on, Occar!"

Oscar stayed behind for a minute to look at Mr. Morrow's paintings of the farm. There was their barn that had survived the fire. There were the golden wheat fields that Papa had carved out of the wild prairie. There was their little house, where Oscar and Mama and Papa had been so happy. There was the front porch, where Mama and Mr. Morrow had sat talking and laughing late into the night.

And that's when it hit Oscar: He could keep his promise to Papa. Every day he could look at

Mr. Morrow's paintings. He could watch over the farm from here. And he would look out these windows to watch as Chicago sprouted up again.

But now it was time to go downstairs with Jennie and Bruno, to join Mama and Mr. Morrow.

Finally Bruno would get his cookie.

WALKING IN OSCAR'S FOOTSTEPS

Every I Survived book feels like a special occasion for me, a chance to travel back in time, to bring new characters to life. But this book, the eleventh in the I Survived series, is unique because the topic was picked by you, my readers. Thousands of I Survived readers participated in an online contest in which you chose one of three topics.

The winner: the Great Chicago Fire.

And now can I tell you a little secret? (Don't tell my editor!)

I wasn't *really* rooting for the Chicago Fire to win. Of course I knew it was a terrible disaster. But

I worried that it wouldn't be so interesting to write about.

Well, I was wrong. And that's what I LOVE about writing this series. Even topics that at first don't fascinate me get a grip on me, pull me in, take over my thoughts.

The Chicago Historical Society has collected eyewitness accounts by survivors, and most are available online. There are also some incredible books about the history of Chicago, and I devoured them. I studied old maps and hundreds of photographs, and watched documentaries.

But the best part of researching my book was visiting Chicago with my family.

What a beautiful city! We prowled the streets, staring at some of the most famous skyscrapers in the world. We took a boat ride along the Chicago River, strolled the shores of Lake Michigan, and gorged ourselves on some of the most delicious foods I have ever eaten.

I was able to imagine the city as Oscar would have seen it in 1871. It wasn't such a pretty place back then. The streets were crowded with buggies and wagons and drays, all pulled by horses. The wooden sidewalks were raised above the streets, so you had to be careful not to tumble off. Hundreds of trains arrived in Chicago every day, more than in any other city in the world. Train tracks ran right along the streets, and grisly collisions between trains and wagons, trains and horses, and trains and people were common.

And then there was the smell.

I actually spent about a week coming up with that one line in Chapter 3, where Oscar compares the smell of Chicago to the smell of one hundred skunks in a hot outhouse (I do love a simile!). I'm not sure if that's exactly right, and I'm glad I didn't have to smell it for myself. The stench came from the slaughterhouses, the stockyards filled with cattle, the coal smoke from factories and hundreds of trains steaming in and out every day. Plus, people didn't take as many baths back then, or wash their clothes often. So you can imagine (or better yet, maybe you shouldn't try!).

But even in those long-ago smelly days, Chicago inspired people with its unique energy and can-do spirit. Many of those who lived in Chicago at the time of the fire were new immigrants, most from Germany, Poland, and Ireland. They had braved long voyages in hopes of finding better lives for their families.

It was this spirit that made Chicago into the fastest-growing city in the world, and that enabled its people to rebound from the Great Fire. Just two decades after that terrible disaster, Chicago had been completely rebuilt, and this time it truly was beautiful (and better-smelling).

As with every book in my series, the historical events in the story are all true. My characters come from my imagination. But the situations they face and the details of their lives are inspired by real people I discover in my research. I'm grateful to all of you for leading me to this topic, for sending me on a journey through time that I will never forget.

On the following pages are answers to some questions that might be on your mind, and ideas for how you can learn more on your own.

Lauren Tarshis

QUESTIONS AND ANSWERS ABOUT THE GREAT CHICAGO FIRE AND MORE

When did the fire start, and how long did it last?

The fire began at around 9:00 P.M. on Sunday, October 8, 1871. It started in a barn owned by the O'Leary family, on DeKoven Street. It spread quickly to the north and east, crossing the river, and finally destroying an area of the city four miles long and one mile wide. The worst of the fires had burned themselves out by late Monday night. Rain that started on Tuesday morning finished the job.

What about Mrs. O'Leary and her cow?

The most famous story about the Chicago Fire tells how it started. It goes like this: A poor and lazy woman named Catherine O'Leary was in her barn on Sunday night, milking the cow she'd ignored all day. The cow was upset and kicked over a kerosene lamp that Mrs. O'Leary had brought into the barn to light her way. *Whoosh!* The fire started, and burned much of Chicago to the ground.

This story was first printed in the Chicago *Evening Journal–Extra* on Monday, October 9, while the fire still raged. The story spread as quickly as the fire.

The only problem with the story: It's probably not true.

Catherine O'Leary was a real woman. Her cow was a real cow, and there is no doubt that the fire started in her barn.

But most agree that the rest of the story is fiction. Even the man who wrote the newspaper article admitted he'd made up the part about the cow kicking over the lamp. He was looking for a colorful story to explain how the great fire started, and people were eager to pin the blame on someone. Poor Mrs. O'Leary.

Here is what is known for sure:

Catherine O'Leary and her husband, Patrick, were a hardworking and respected couple raising six children. Mrs. O'Leary actually had five cows and ran a successful business selling the milk to neighbors. At the time the fire started, at around 9:00, the O'Learys were fast asleep. But the truth didn't matter. As Jim Murphy wrote in *The Great Fire*, "Gossip hardened into established fact."

The O'Learys lost all of their cows in the fire. But it was the gossip that did the most damage. According to her children, Mrs. O'Leary never recovered from the hurt and shame of being unfairly blamed for the most famous fire in U.S. history.

So who is to blame for starting the fire?

Over the years, people have suggested other theories about the cause of the fire. Some blame people who were renting the small cottage near the O'Learys' house. There were reports that they hosted a party, and that guests drifted into the barn and sparked the fire with their pipes or cigars. Others blame a man named Daniel "Peg Leg" Sullivan, claiming that he might have sneaked into the barn to steal some milk.

But there is no evidence backing up these theories.

The real causes are probably less interesting.

The main culprit was a drought that had gripped the entire Midwest for more than a year before the fire. In Chicago, only one inch of rain had fallen since early July. The entire city was bone dry.

Another cause, and probably more important, was the careless way the city had been built. Most buildings were made of wood, mostly pine, which is especially flammable. Even most of the "fireproof" buildings were often made of wood, with thin layers or brick or marble on top and highly flammable tar shingles covering their rooftops. The city's miles of sidewalks were made of wood, as were many roads. In some neighborhoods, wooden houses, shacks, and barns were all crammed together.

Did people know this was dangerous? Yes. Fires were common in cities back then. But in the fastest-growing city on earth, these worries were pushed to the side.

Why didn't the fire department try harder to put the fire out?

Chicago really did have one of the best fire departments in the country, with 185 firefighters and 17 horse-drawn steam engines. These engines, powered by coal, were used to pump water through hoses.

Just the night before, the fire department had battled an enormous blaze not far from the O'Learys. It took nearly every fireman in the city to fight that fire, which destroyed dozens of buildings. But in the end, the firemen succeeded in putting it out before it spread farther.

It was these same exhausted, scorched firemen who were called to fight the fire that broke out in the O'Learys' barn. Seven fire companies rushed out. But a series of errors sent them to the wrong neighborhood. By the time they arrived at the scene, the blaze was out of control and was spraying embers and sparks into the sky. An unusually strong wind was blowing that night, and it carried those sparks far and wide, igniting fires and then spreading the flames.

How many people died?

Estimates hover around 300. At the time, about 334,000 people lived in Chicago, so the vast majority of the residents did manage to escape. Many of those who died were trapped by the fire. Others died crossing bridges that collapsed into the Chicago River.

Was the Chicago Fire the deadliest in U.S. history?

The Great Chicago Fire is remembered because it destroyed a four-mile swath of one of America's most important cities. But it was not the deadliest fire. Amazingly the deadliest fire in U.S. history happened the *very same day* as the Great Chicago Fire, about 250 miles to the north, in Peshtigo, Wisconsin.

Peshtigo was a logging town, and workers often set small fires in the surrounding forests to burn away brush and stumps. But on October 8, those same prairie winds that hit Chicago were blowing in Peshtigo, and the small fires turned into a massive forest fire.

Nobody knows exactly how many people died in the Peshtigo fire — between 1,500 and 2,500. But the terrible event was overshadowed by the Chicago disaster.

Were there really children living alone like Jennie and Bruno?

Sadly, yes. In fact, this is the second I Survived book that features children who are orphaned and living on the streets (the other is *I Survived the San Francisco Earthquake, 1906*). The problem of "street children" was huge in American cities, until perhaps the 1930s. Many children lost their parents to diseases that today are curable, such as cholera and influenza. In Jennie and Bruno's day, many children also had lost their fathers on the battlefields of the Civil War, which ended in 1865.

What happened to people who survived the fire?

Of the 334,000 people living in Chicago at the time of the fire, 100,000 lost their homes.

Within days of the fire, train cars filled with food, tents, clothes, blankets, and other supplies were pouring into Chicago from all around the country. Tent cities cropped up in Lincoln Park. The city set up food kitchens, and handed out wood so people could build shacks where their houses had stood.

But life was grim and difficult, especially for the poor. Many people lost everything they owned in the fire. And with so many factories and businesses destroyed, many people could not find jobs.

But most people in the city were determined to rebuild their lives — and their city.

By the early 1880s, the city was bustling again. Glorious new buildings replaced the shoddily constructed structures that had burned so quickly in the fire. Strict building laws made the people living there much safer.

FOR FURTHER READING AND LEARNING

I used many books and other resources to research my book. Here are two I think you would like to explore on your own.

The Great Chicago Fire and the Web of Memory

This website, created by the Chicago Historical Society and Northwestern University, features eyewitness accounts of the fire, articles written in the aftermath, photographs and illustrations from the time of the Great Chicago Fire, and

much more. You could spend weeks happily exploring this interactive site.
www.greatchicagofire.org

The Great Fire by Jim Murphy
(Scholastic)
In this award-winning book for kids, author Jim Murphy follows a group of survivors of the Chicago Fire to create an almost minute-by-minute account of the event, from the first sparks in the O'Leary barn to the city's recovery.